D0577065

BOOK CLUB EDITION

INSIDE

OUTSIDE

UPSIDE DOWN

by Stan and Jan Berenstain

A Bright & Early Book

RANDOM HOUSE / NEW YORK

Copyright © 1968 by Stanley and Janice Berenstain. All rights reserved under International and Pan-American Copyright Conventions. Published in the United States by Random House, Inc., New York, and simultaneously in Canada by Random House of Canada Limited, Toronto. Library of Congress Catalog Card Number: 68-28465. Manufactured in the United States of America.

D   E   F   G   H   I   J   K

3   4

Going in

Inside

Inside a box

Upside down

Inside a box
Upside down

Going out

Outside

Outside
Inside a box
Upside down

Going on

On a truck
Outside
Inside a box
Upside down

Going

Going to town
On a truck
Outside
Inside a box
Upside down

Falling off

Off the truck

Coming out

Right side up!

Mama! Mama!
I went to town.
Inside,
Outside,
Upside down!